For Audrey, Frank, Liz, Janice,
Rebecca, Sarah and Ulla —
the Andersen Team.

Copyright © 2005 by David McKee
The rights of David McKee to be identified as the author and illustrator of this work
have been asserted by him in accordance with the Copyright, Designs and Patents Act, 1988.
First published in Great Britain in 2005 by Andersen Press Ltd, 20 Vauxhall Bridge Road,
London SW1V 2SA. Published in Australia by Random House Australia Pty.,
20 Alfred Street, Milsons Point, Sydney, NSW 2061. All rights reserved.
Colour separated in Switzerland by Photolitho AG, Zürich.
Printed and bound in Italy by Grafiche AZ, Verona.

10   9   8   7   6   5   4   3   2   1

British Library Cataloguing in Publication Data available.

ISBN 1 84270 385 4

This book has been printed on acid-free paper

THREE MONSTERS

David McKee

Andersen Press
London

There were once two monsters who lived in a place
between the sea and the jungle; a place covered with rocks.
Every day, one monster would say,
"We should get rid of these rocks."
And every day, the other monster would reply,
"Yes. Tomorrow, perhaps." Then they would laugh.
They were very lazy monsters.

One day, as they were looking out to sea,
the first monster said, "Look! A boat."
"With something in it," said the other.

The boat came closer and closer and finally landed.
Out stepped a yellow monster.
"Yuk!" said the two monsters together.

"Oh, Most Honourable and Handsome Worships,"
   said the yellow monster. "An earthquake has destroyed
   my land. I seek a place to live."
"Not here, you custard-coloured, cringing creep,"
   said the first monster. "Push off."

"Oh, Glorious Kindnesses, just a little space, please,"
said the yellow monster. "I can be useful to your
Wonderfulnesses."
"Clear off," shouted the second monster. "We don't want
any funny foreigner types here."

"Wait a minute," whispered the first monster. "He said 'useful'." Then to the yellow monster he said, "Hang about there, Mustard-face."

The two monsters went behind some rocks to talk. They didn't notice the yellow monster sneak up to listen.

"That yellow moron with his boat can dump the rocks in the sea," said the first monster.
"But he'll want some land in return," said the other monster.

"Naturally," said the first. "And we'll give him land —
the land he's taken away. The rocks."
The yellow monster heard and hurried back to his place.

The two monsters returned. "Right, you yellow-skinned bellyache," said the first. "Clear this place of rocks and we'll give you some land."

"Oh, Royal Wonderfulnesses. Will you really? Monsters' honour?" said the yellow monster.

"Monsters' honour," said the other two together.

The yellow monster set to work at once.
He was very strong.

Meanwhile, the two lazy monsters went to the edge of
the jungle and waited.

Days later, the yellow monster came to them and said,
"Oh, Most Brilliant of Monsters, I've removed the rocks
but the ground is rough. Shall I level it?"
"Obviously," said the second monster. "And tidy the edge
of the jungle."

The yellow monster went back to work,
taking away earth and plants.

Later the yellow monster came again.
"Oh, Most Precious and Honest Royalnesses," he said.
"All is done. Will you now give me the land that you promised?"
"Of course, Gormless Gump," said the first monster.
"A promise is a promise. All the land that you have taken away
   is yours: the rocks, the earth, the plants, everything."

"Oh, joy of joys, wonders of wonders, my very own land,"
   said the yellow monster. "Thank you, Your Magnificences."
   He danced off towards the sea.
   The two monsters stared in surprise.
"Completely bonkers," said the second monster.
   Then they followed him.

When the two monsters reached the sea they saw
the yellow monster in his boat heading for an island.
They stared in surprise.
"That wasn't there before," said the first monster.
"He must have built it from the land we gave him."

"Oi! You canary-coloured wise guy," shouted the second monster. "Can we come and visit you?"

"With pleasure, Your Lovelinesses," called out the yellow monster. "If I can come and visit you!"